HANIMATIONS

Mario Mariotti

ANKY NELL BOOK

Kane/Miller Book Publishers
New York & La Jolla, California

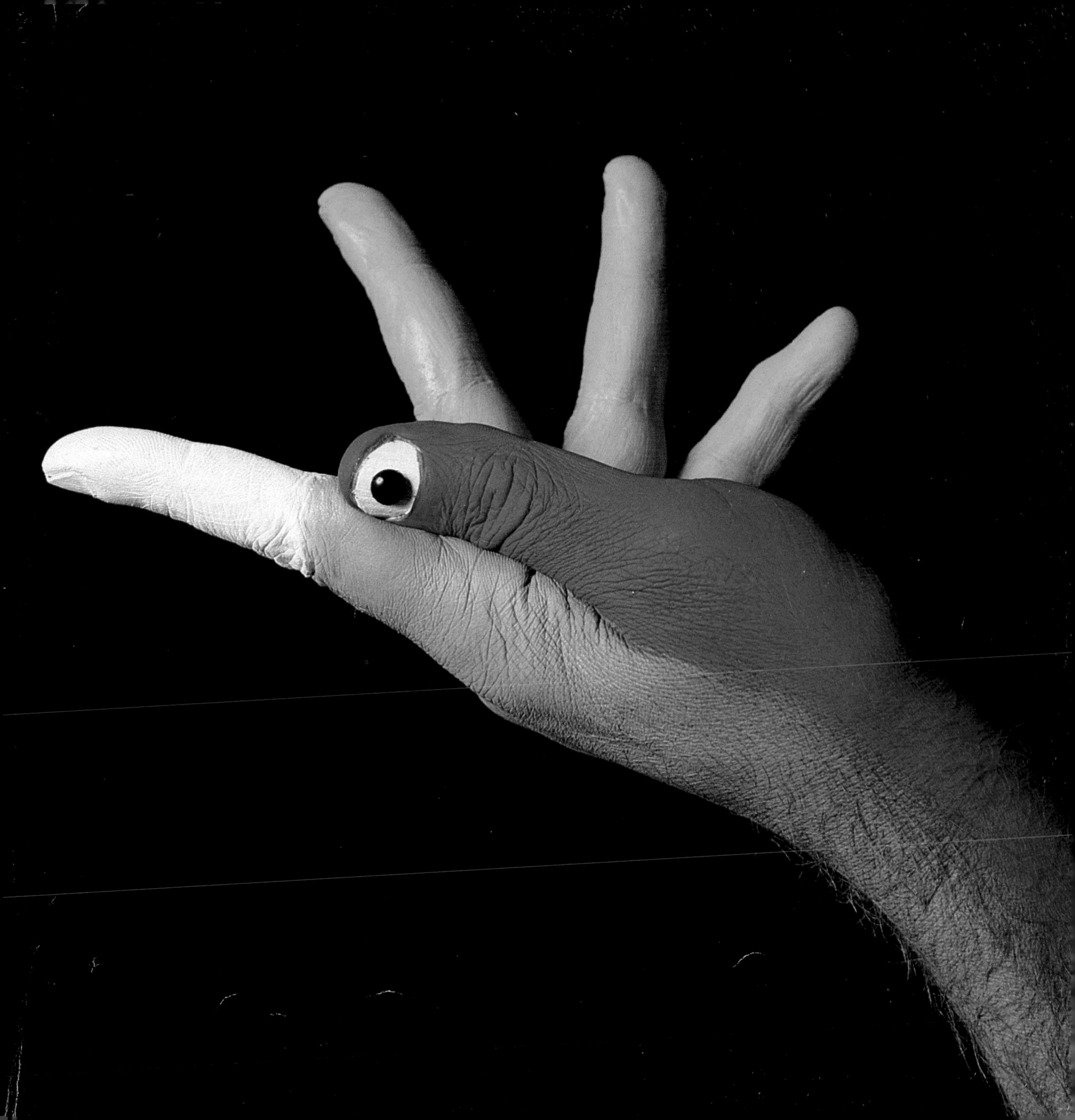

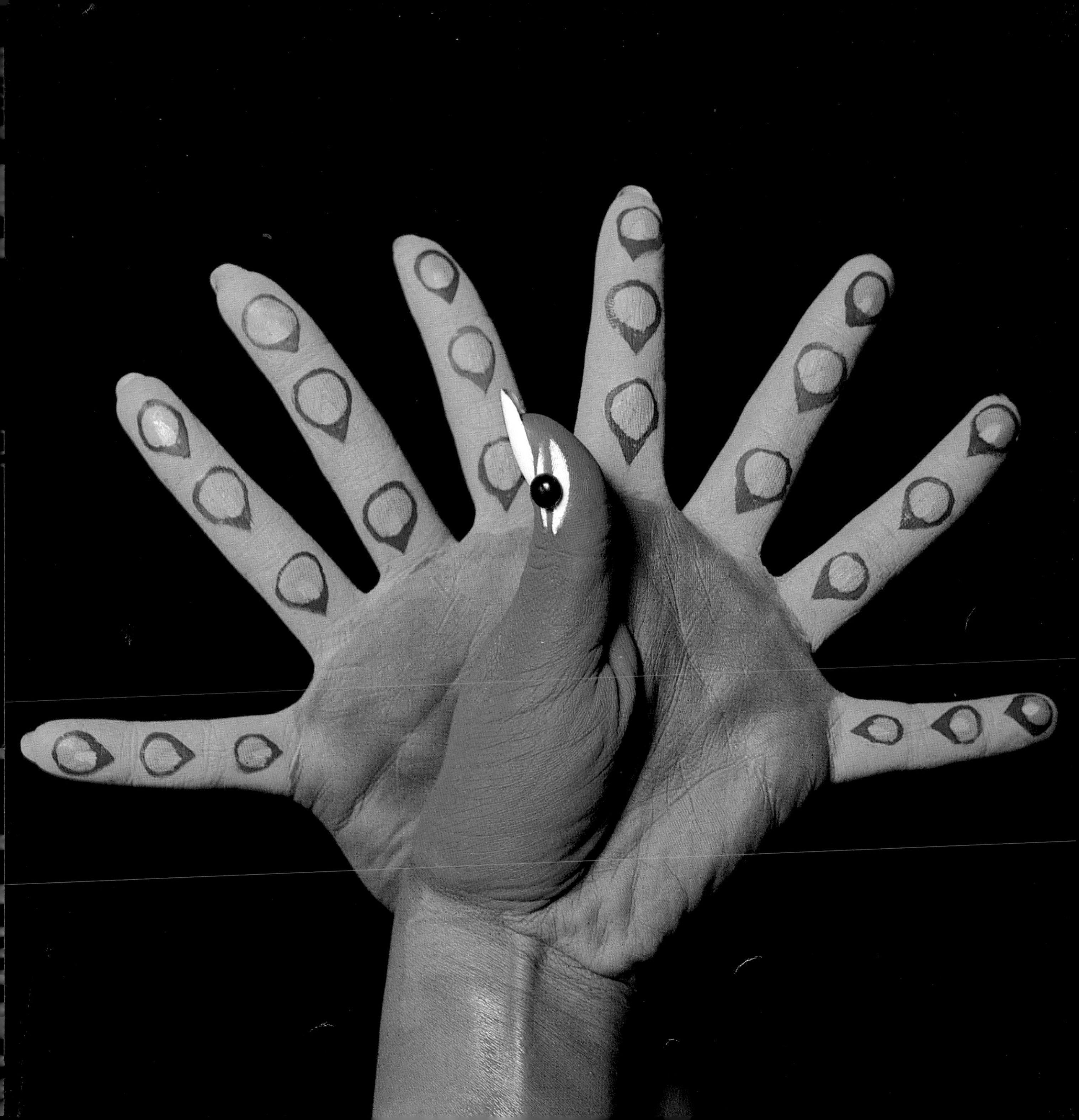

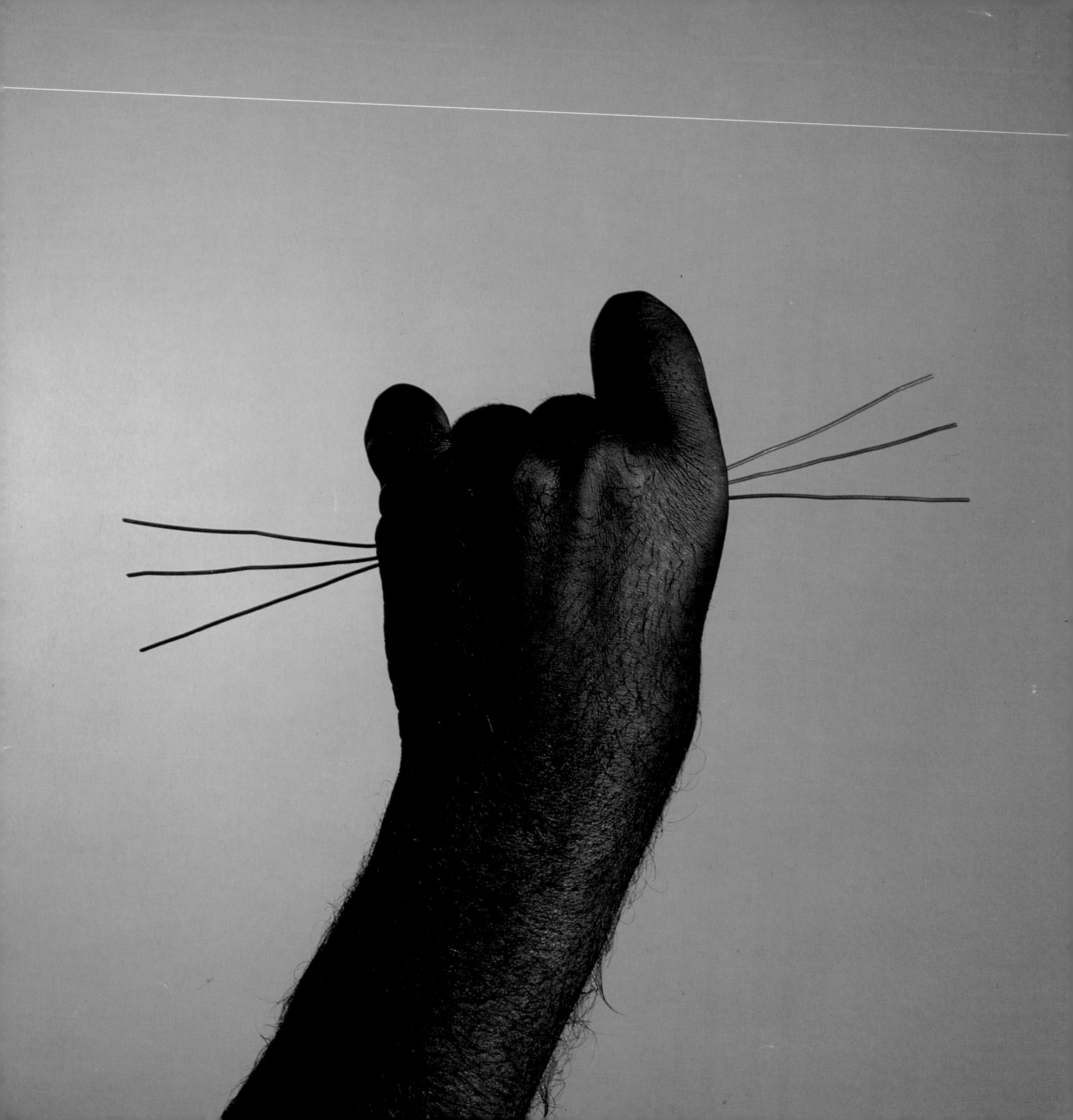

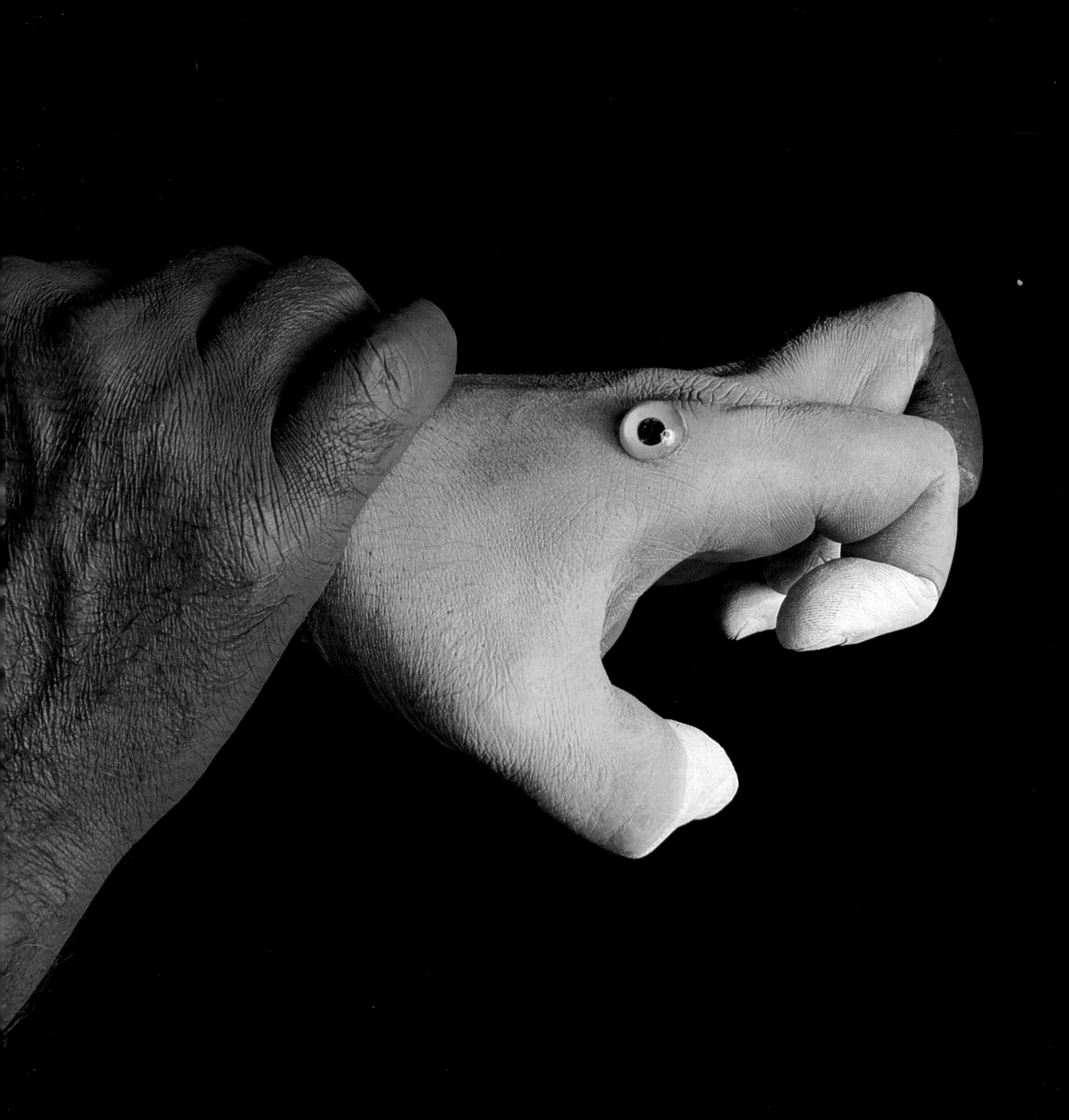

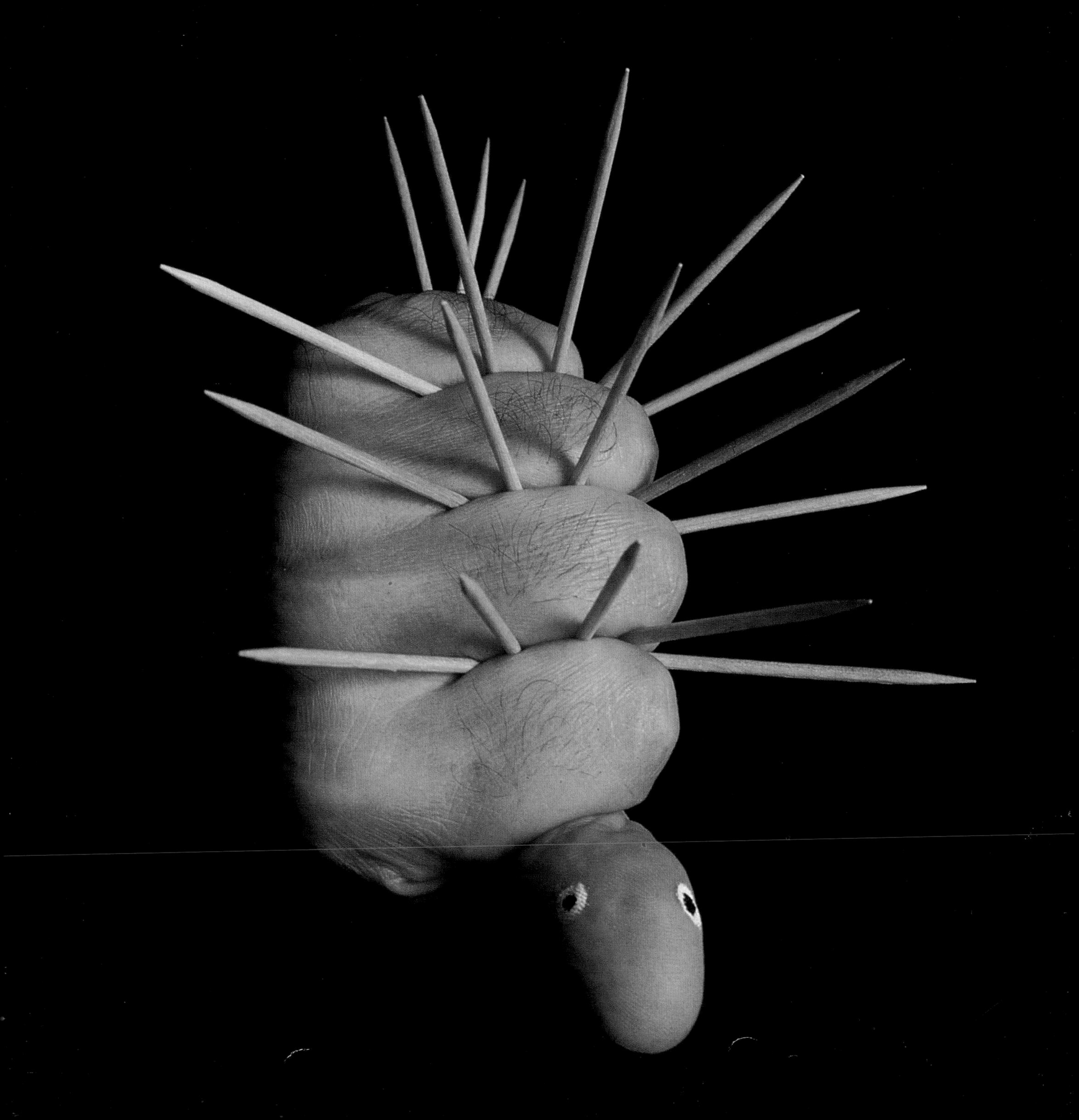

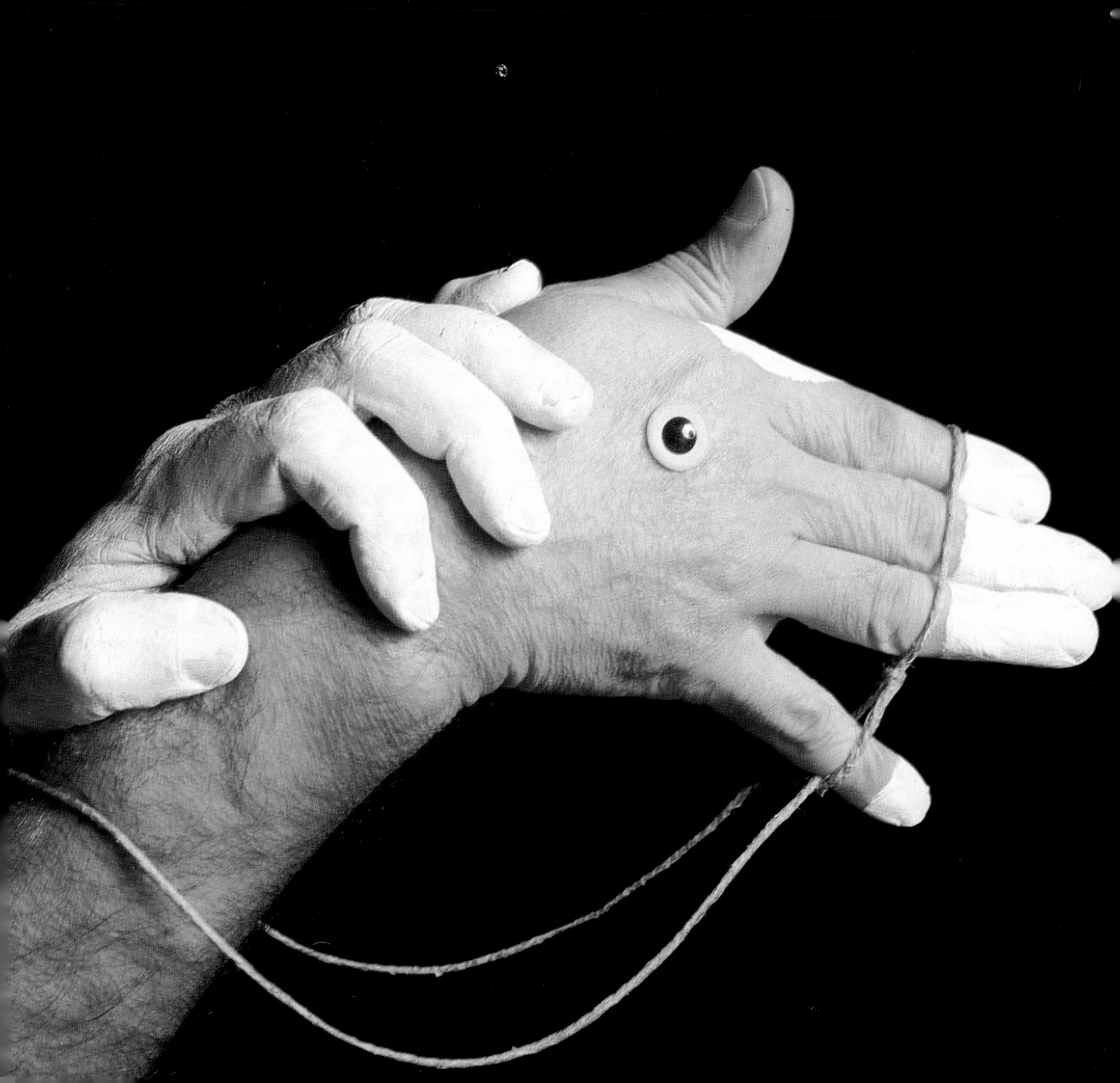

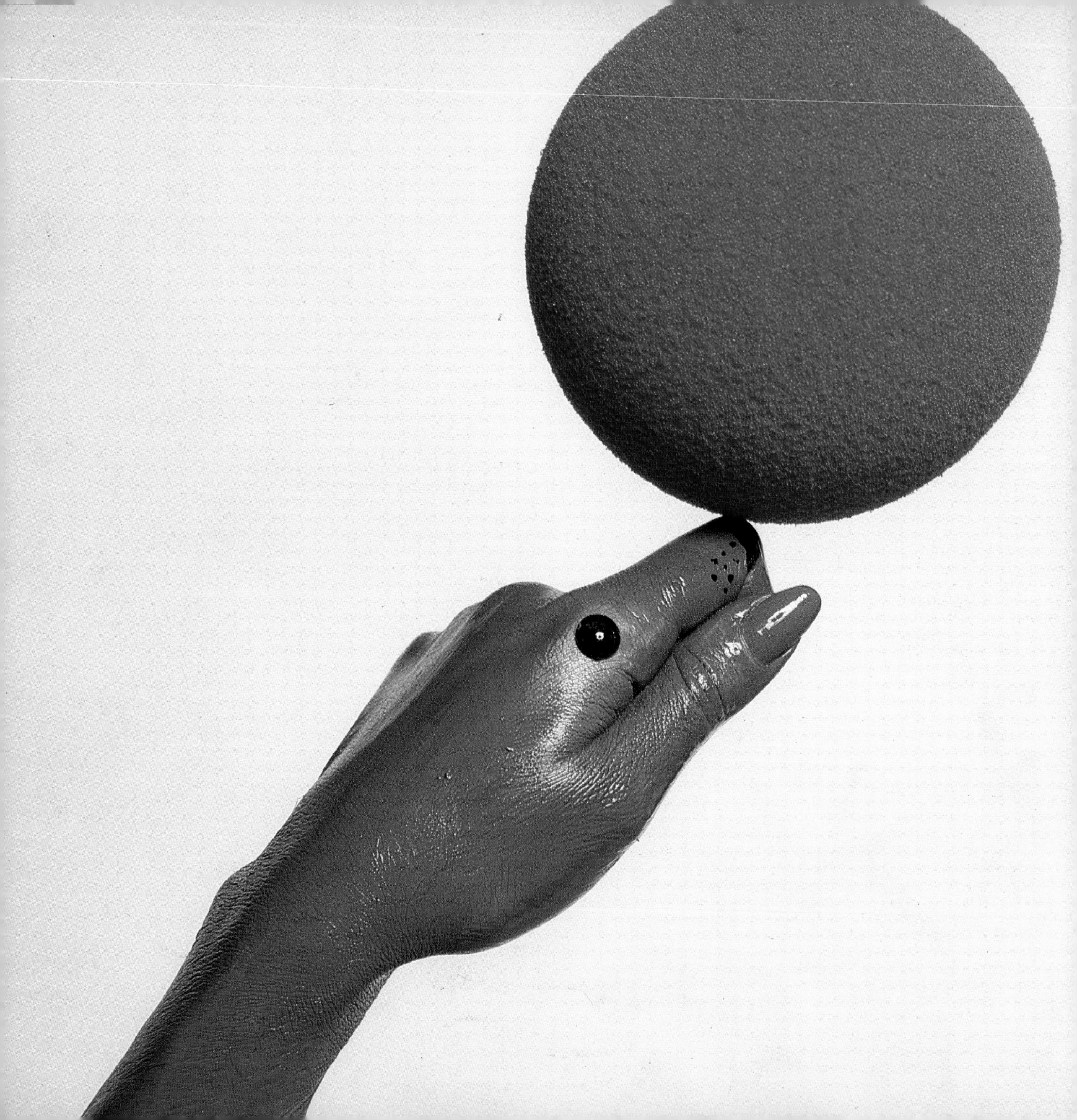

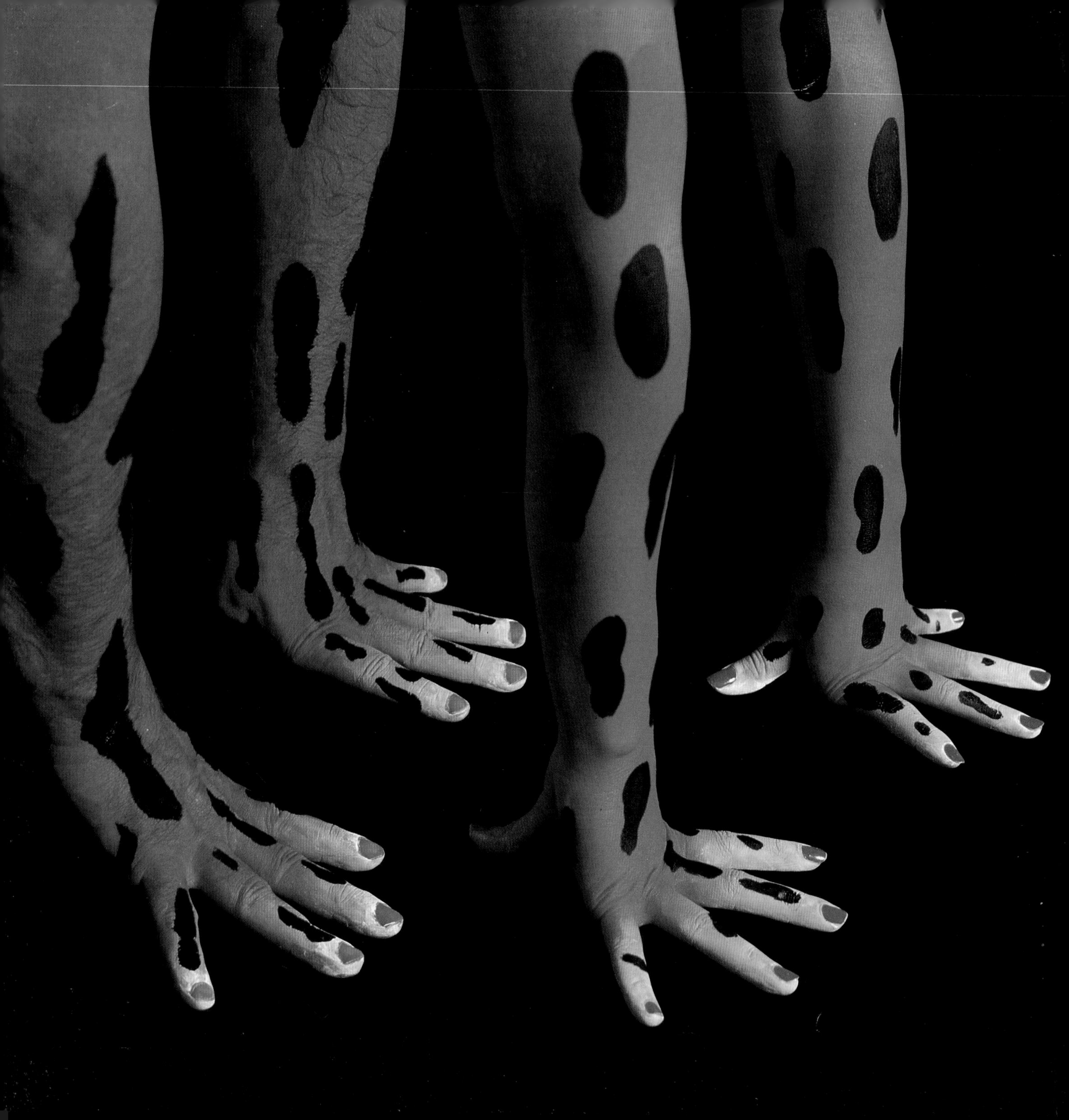

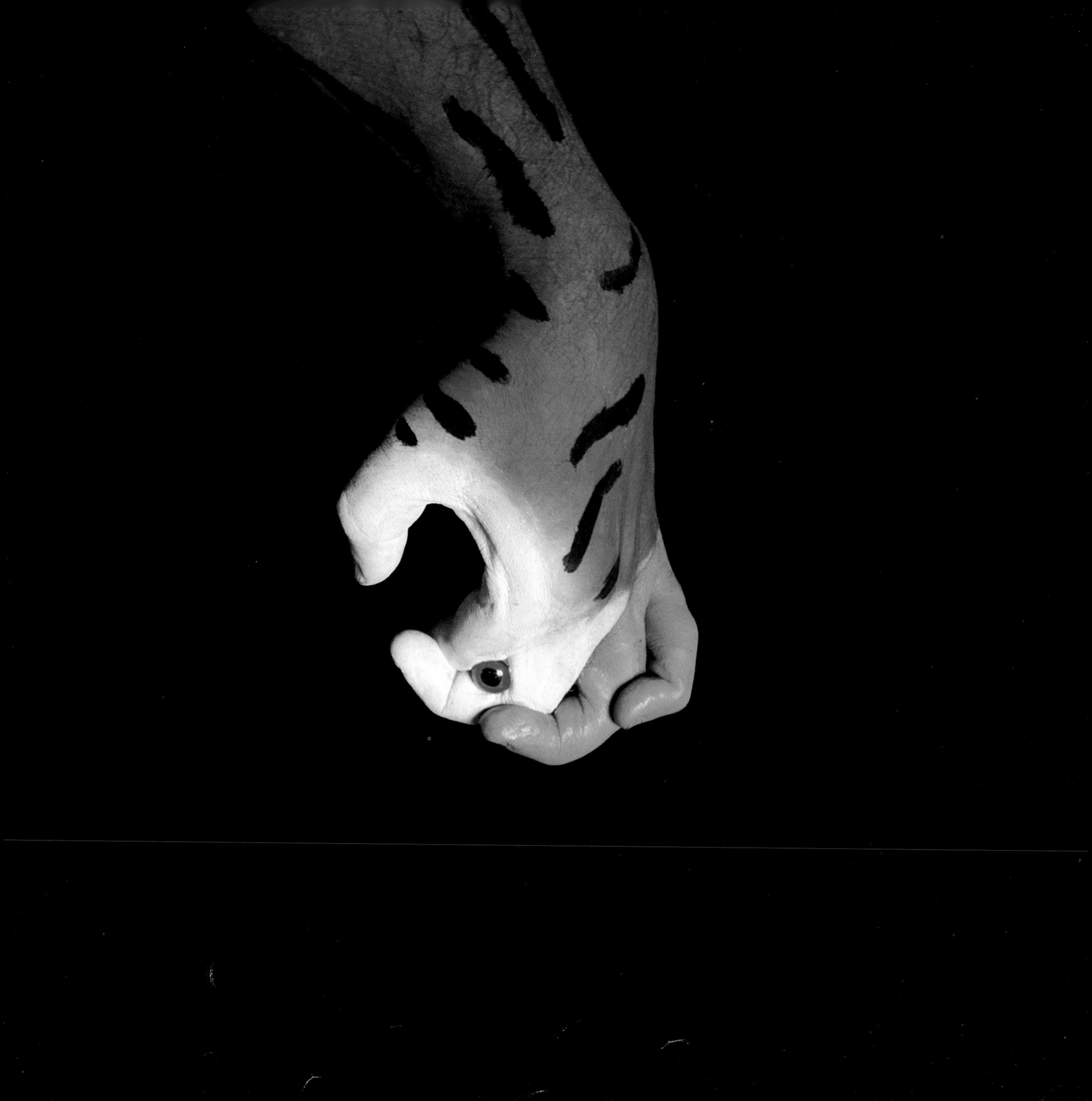

HANIMATIONS continues what I began in my original book HANIMALS. With HANIMATIONS I have not only increased the number of animals but also the number of hands used to create them, for I have added here the hands of my daughter Francesca.

In the years since they were first published, the "Hanimals" have reproduced and multiplied like rabbits. In new editions with new titles in countries near and far, nested between the pages of many small books, they have traveled halfway around the world. Some, the most vain among them, have sneaked their way onto television. Others, the boldest among them, have run off my hand to advertise Japanese watches and other products.

But no matter how far some of my original "Hanimals" may have strayed, they still belong to my original family (though sometimes I wonder). And so too, these "Hanimations" belong to that same family now much enlarged.

Arrivederci!

MARIO MARIOTTI